How to *Draw* for Children and Young Adults

MANGA ART 4

Earl R. Phelps

How To Draw For Children and Young Adults: Manga Art 4

By Earl R. Phelps

Published by Phelps Publishing
P.O. Box 22401
Cleveland, Ohio 44122

ISBN: 978-1-887627-25-2
Printed in the United States of America

www.phelpspublications.com

Table of Contents

Introduction

Hello Artist,

I appreciate you enhancing your art skills with my Manga Art 4 book. You will not only learn how to draw Manga art, but enjoy yourself while doing it. That's what it's all about, having fun. You will learn to draw several different manga characters and I also included some comic book panel pages so you can create your own comic book.

All you need is a pencil and paper to start drawing. You can learn how to draw Manga Art in minutes with these simple step-by-step illustrations. Anyone can learn from this book, from ages 8 to 108. It's all about just putting together circles, squares and lines.

There's no words to this song, you just sing and dance alone, in other words, this book is so simple that the illustrations alone will guide you through everything. No words are needed to explain, just have fun with this drawing game. As the saying goes "A picture is worth a thousand words. "

The key to success is Determination, Persistence, and Practice, Practice and more Practice. Enjoy yourself and let's get Busy!!

Earl R. Phelps

Manga Eyes

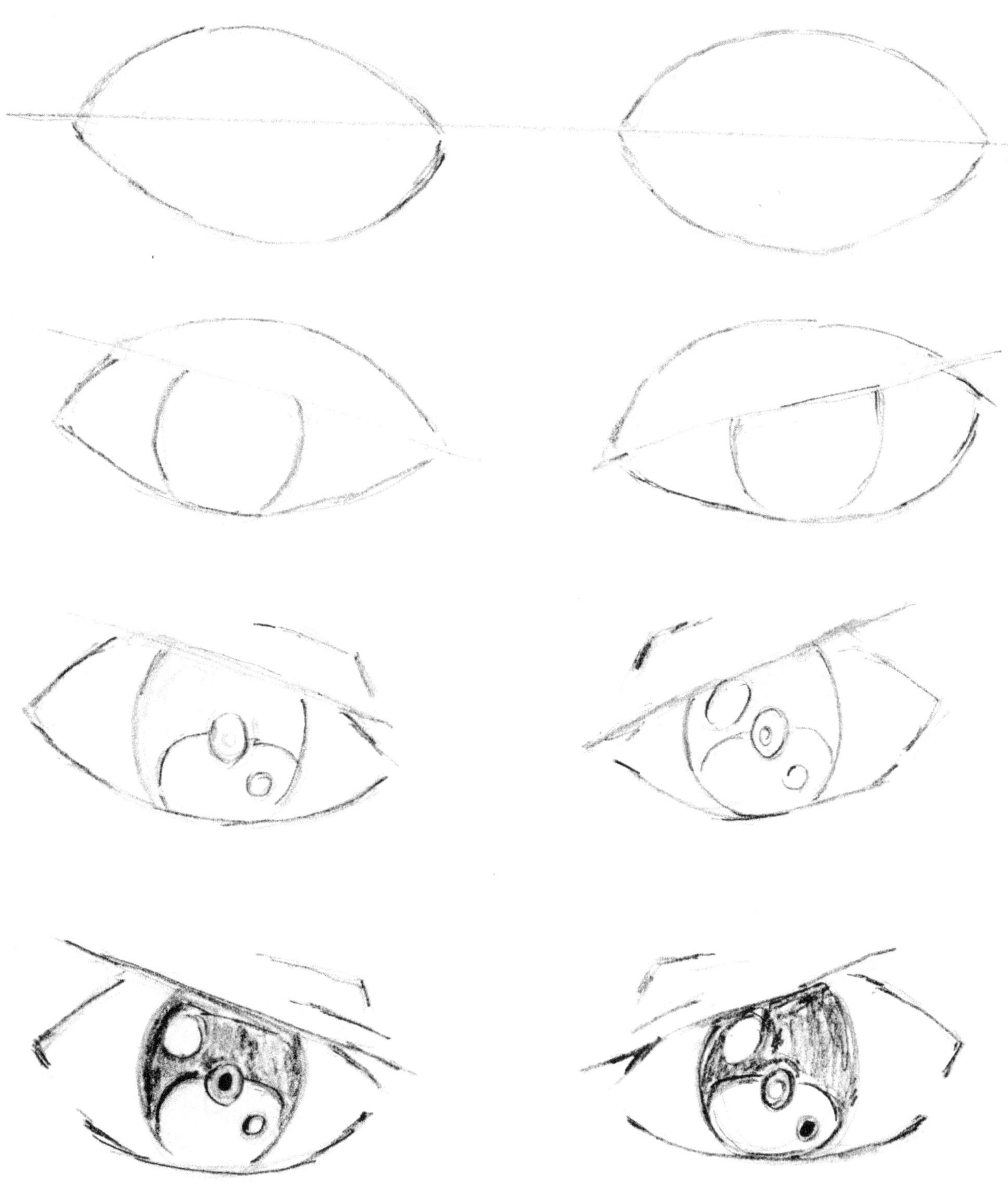

Head Side View

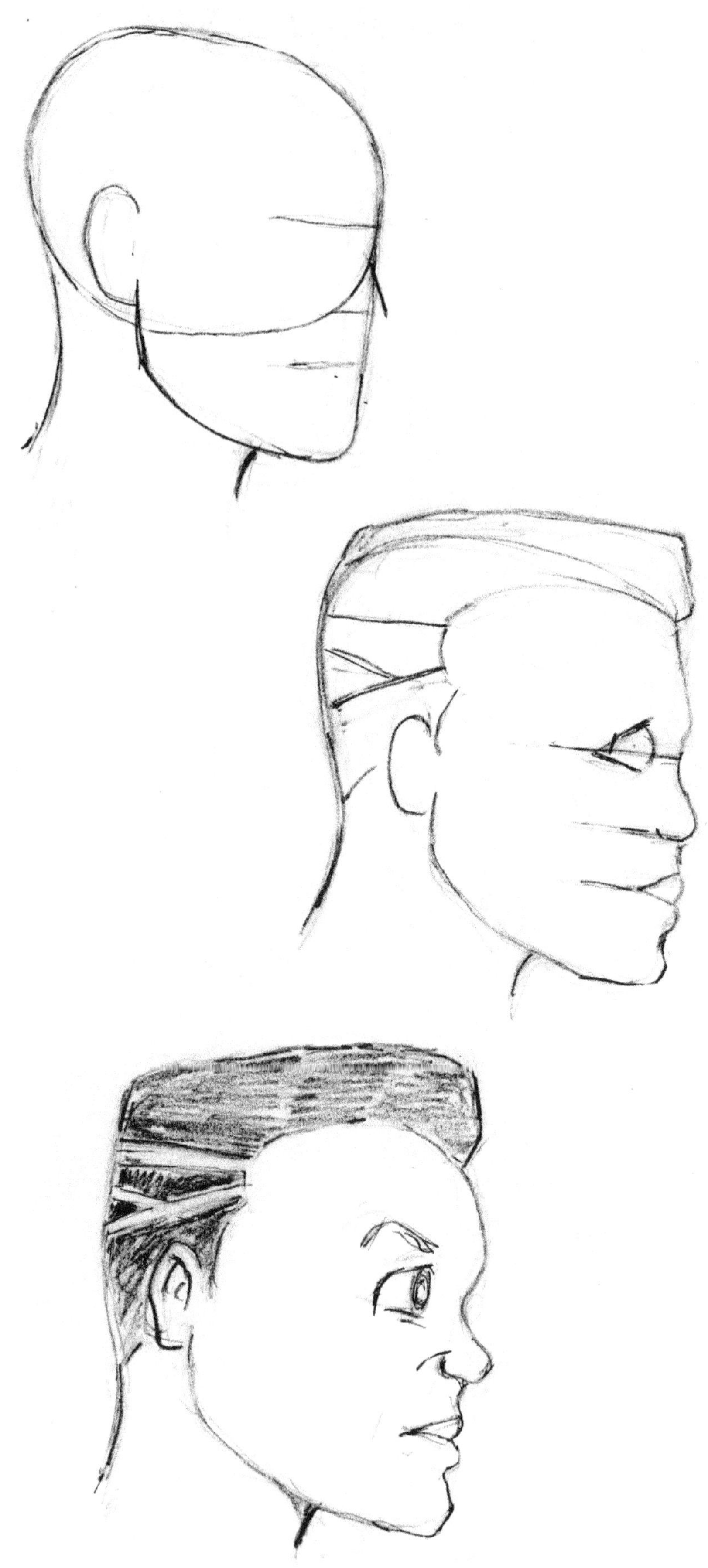

Astro Lightning

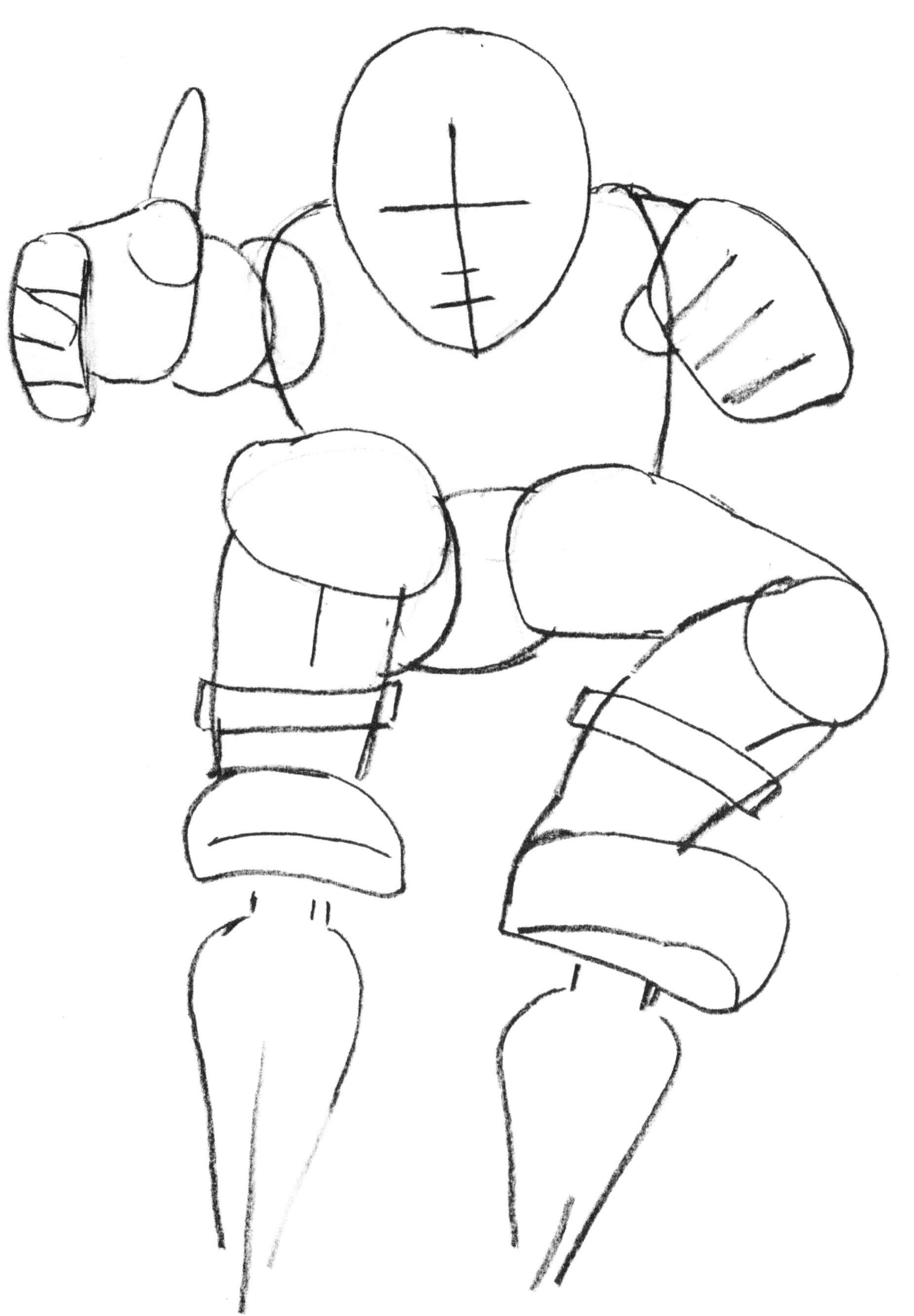

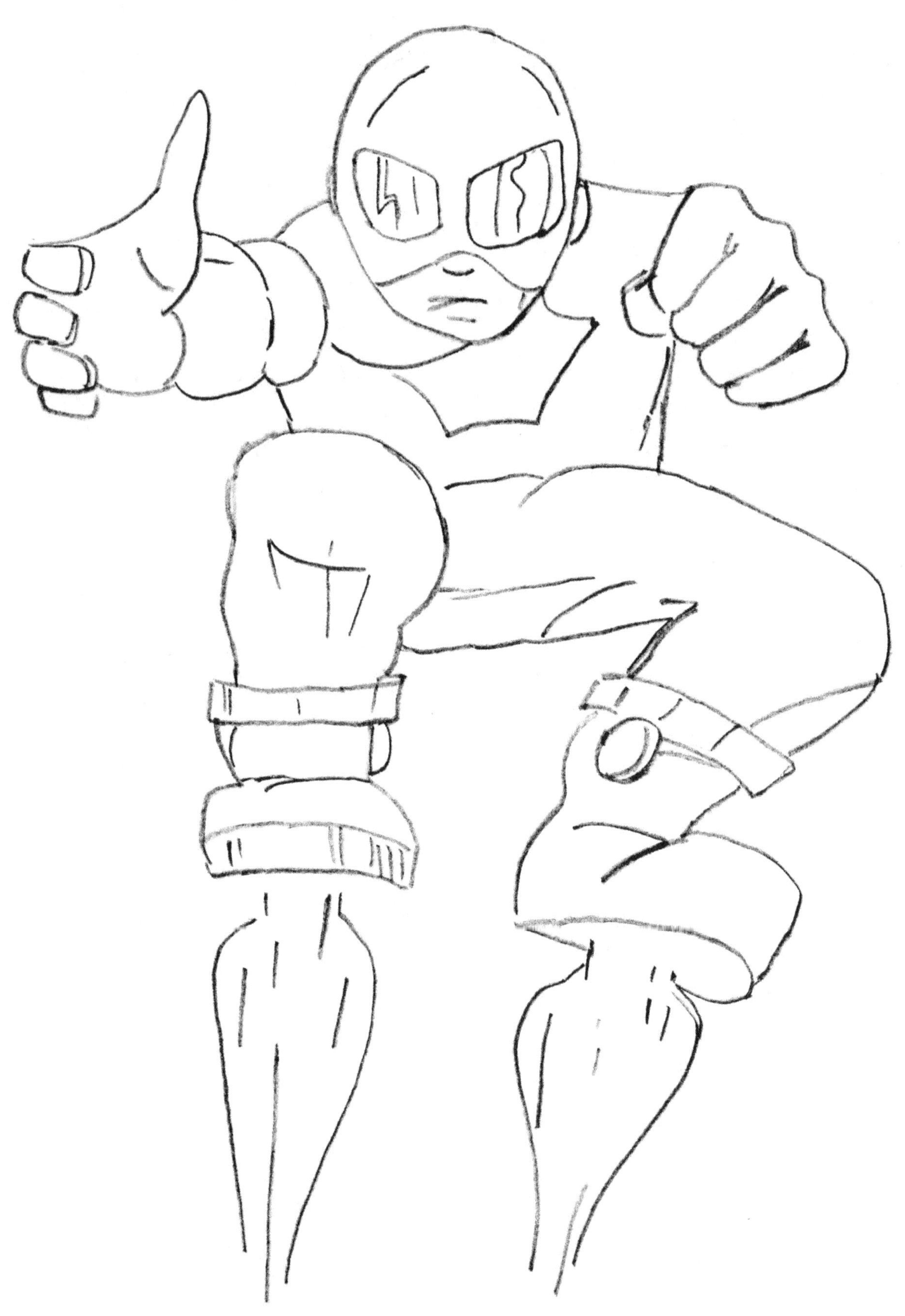

Oogle Boy

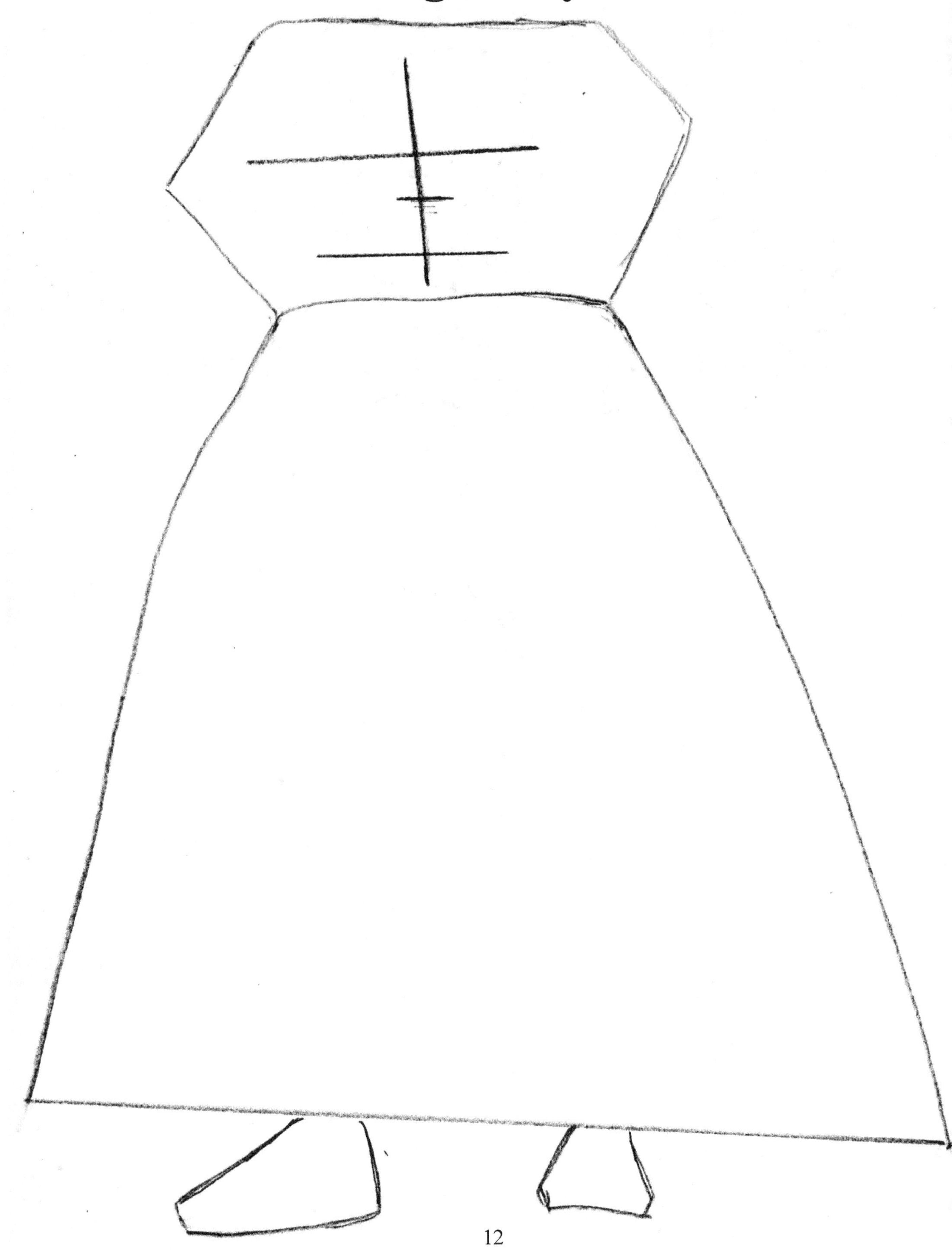

Bag Boy

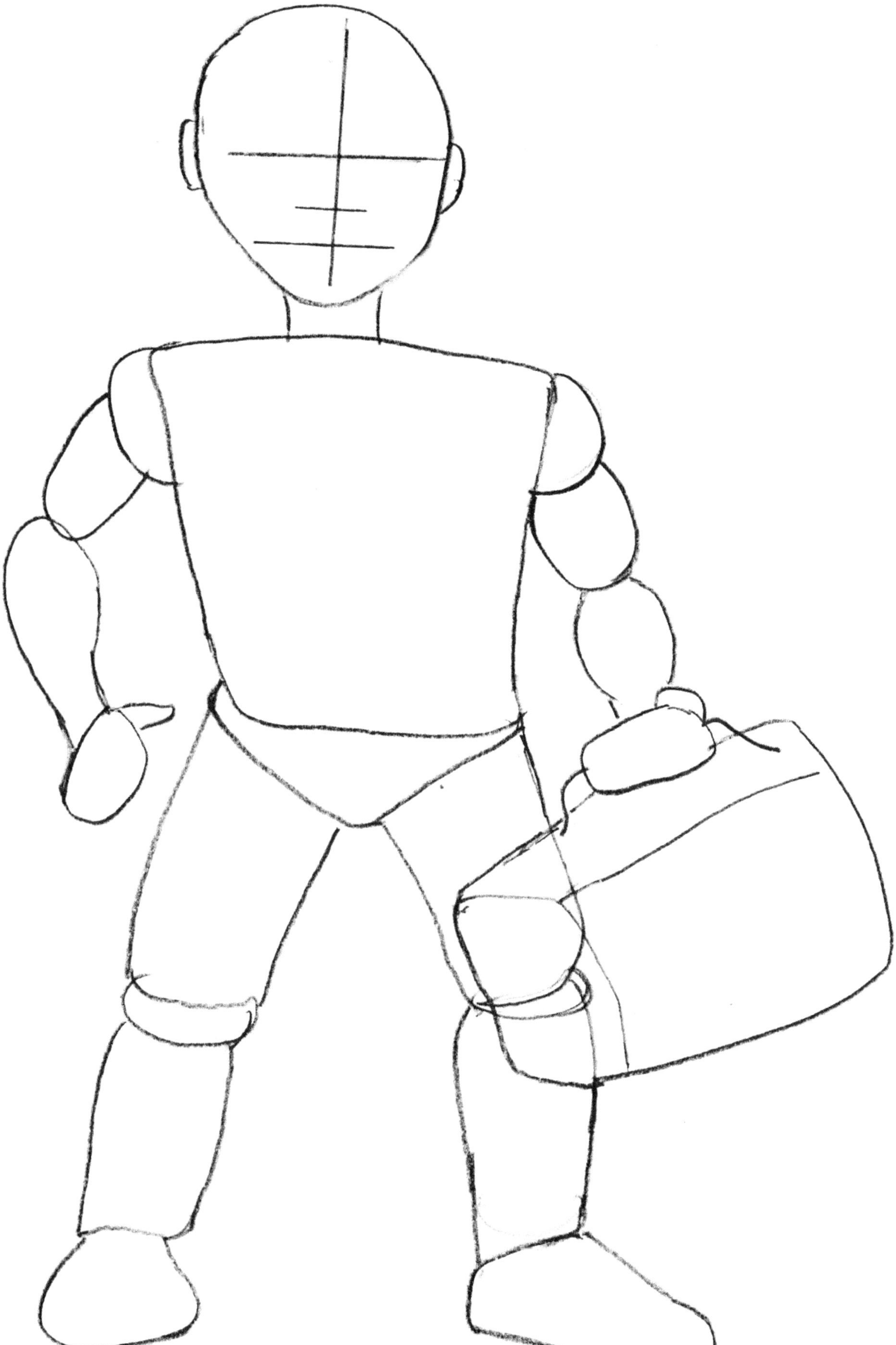

Deano

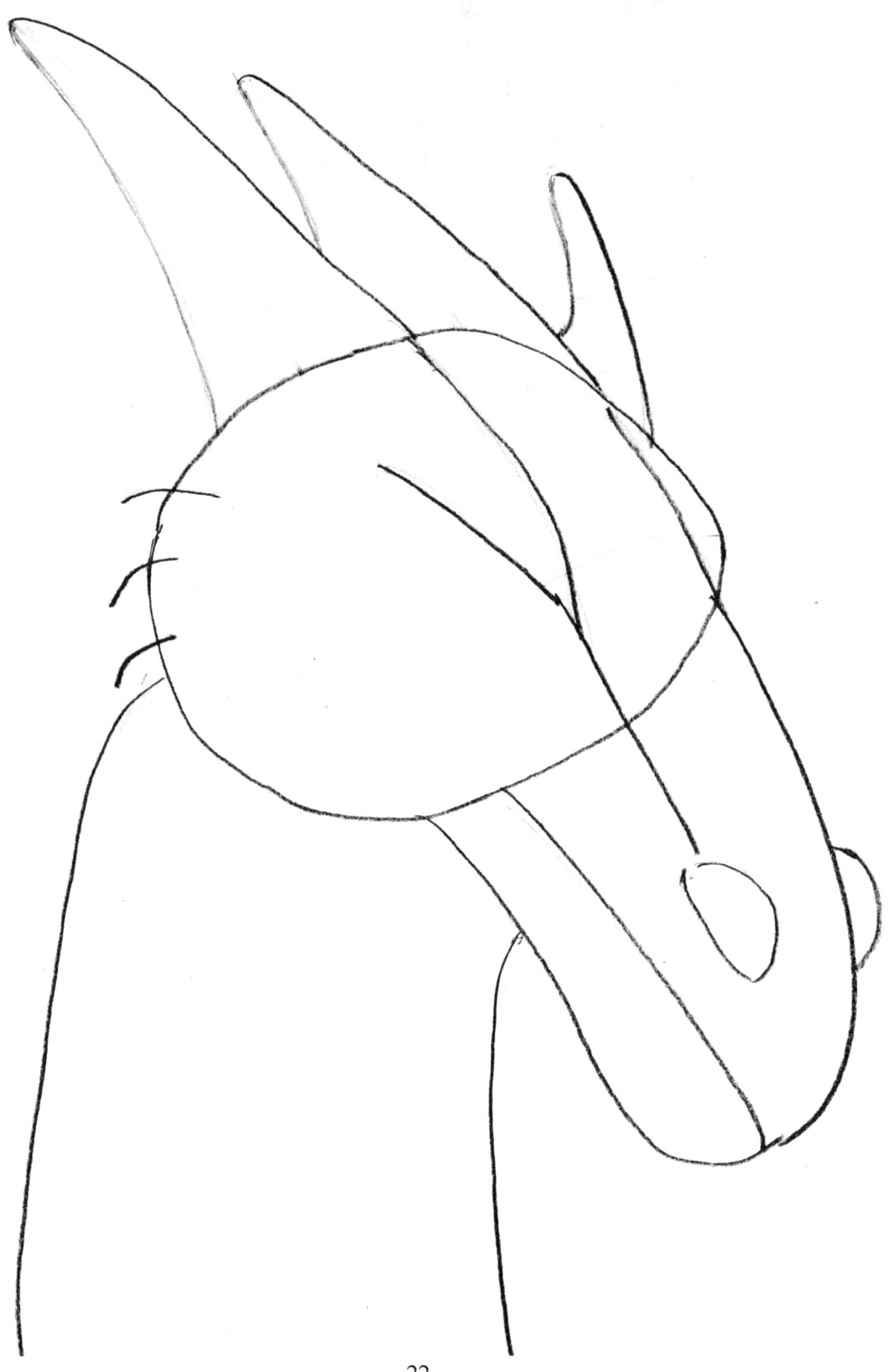

Quadruple Man

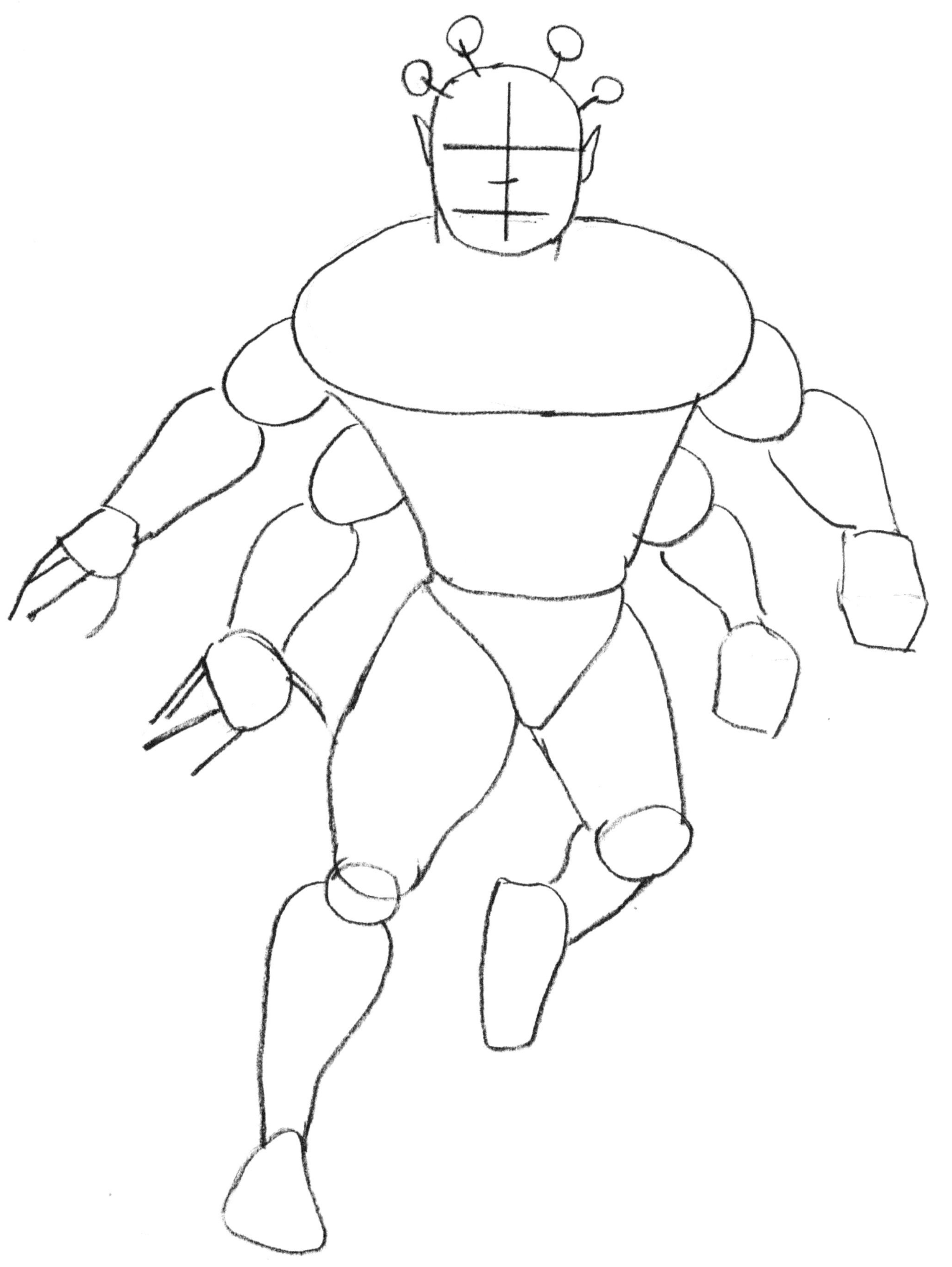

Tornado Kid

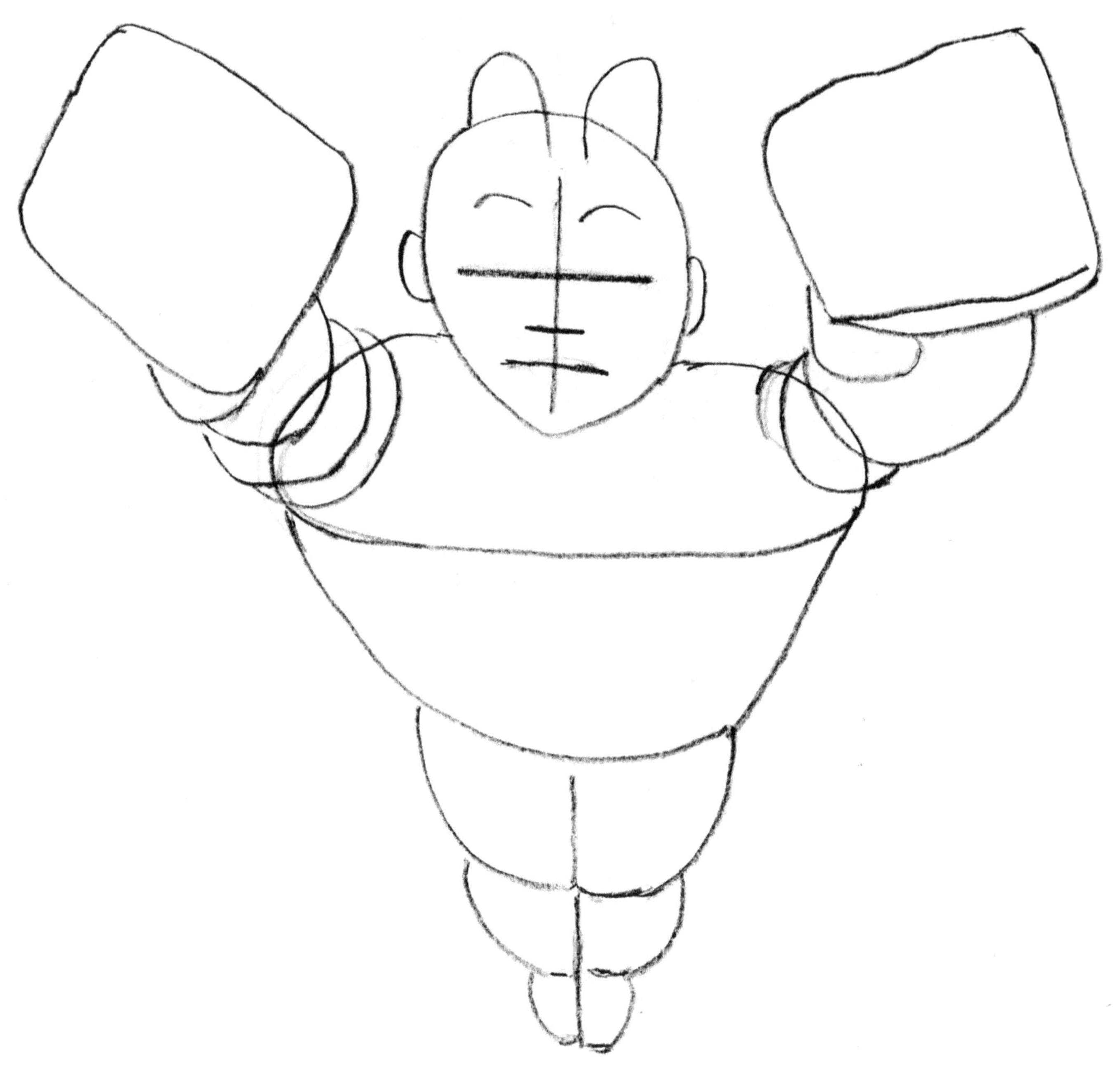

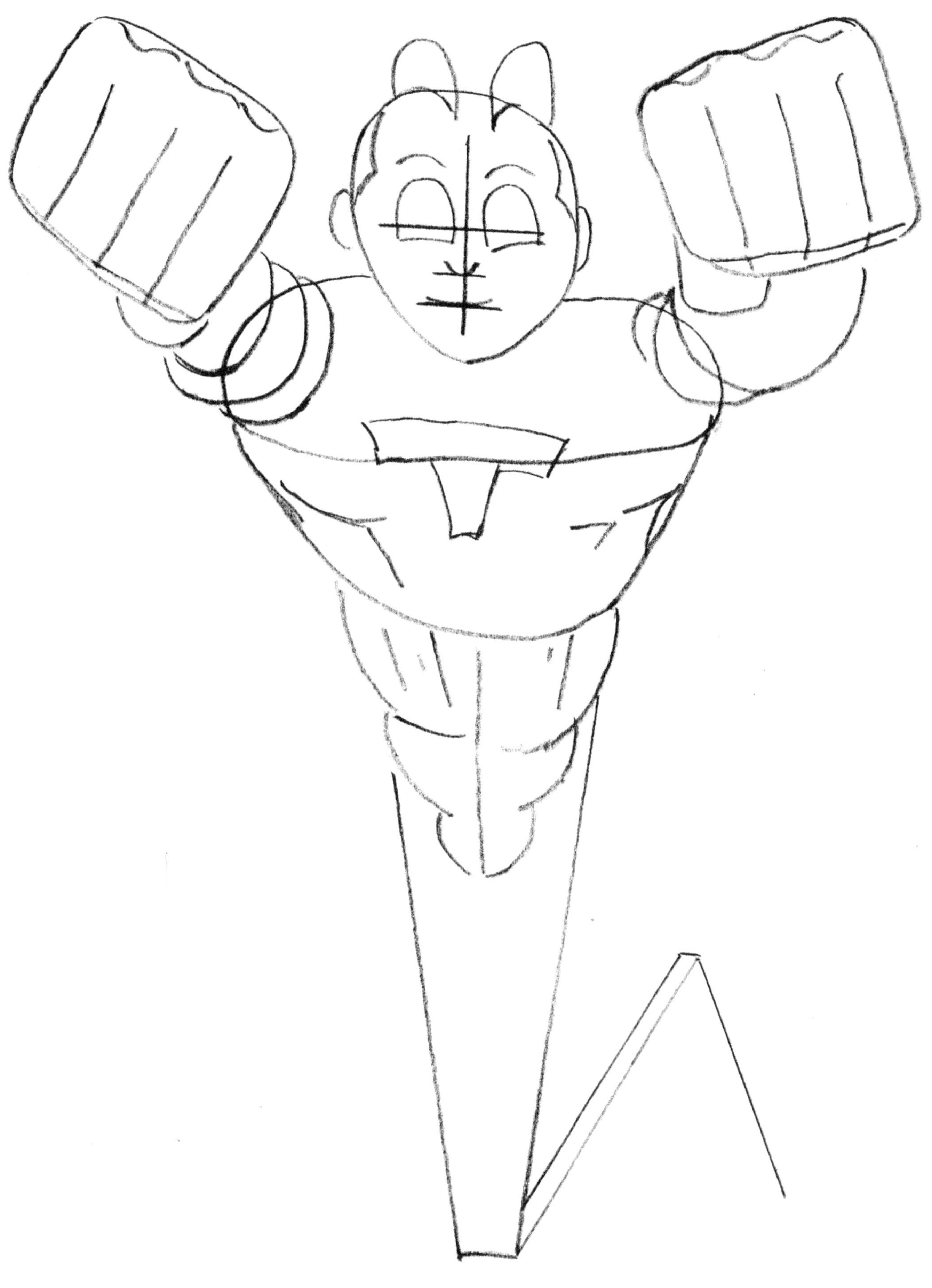

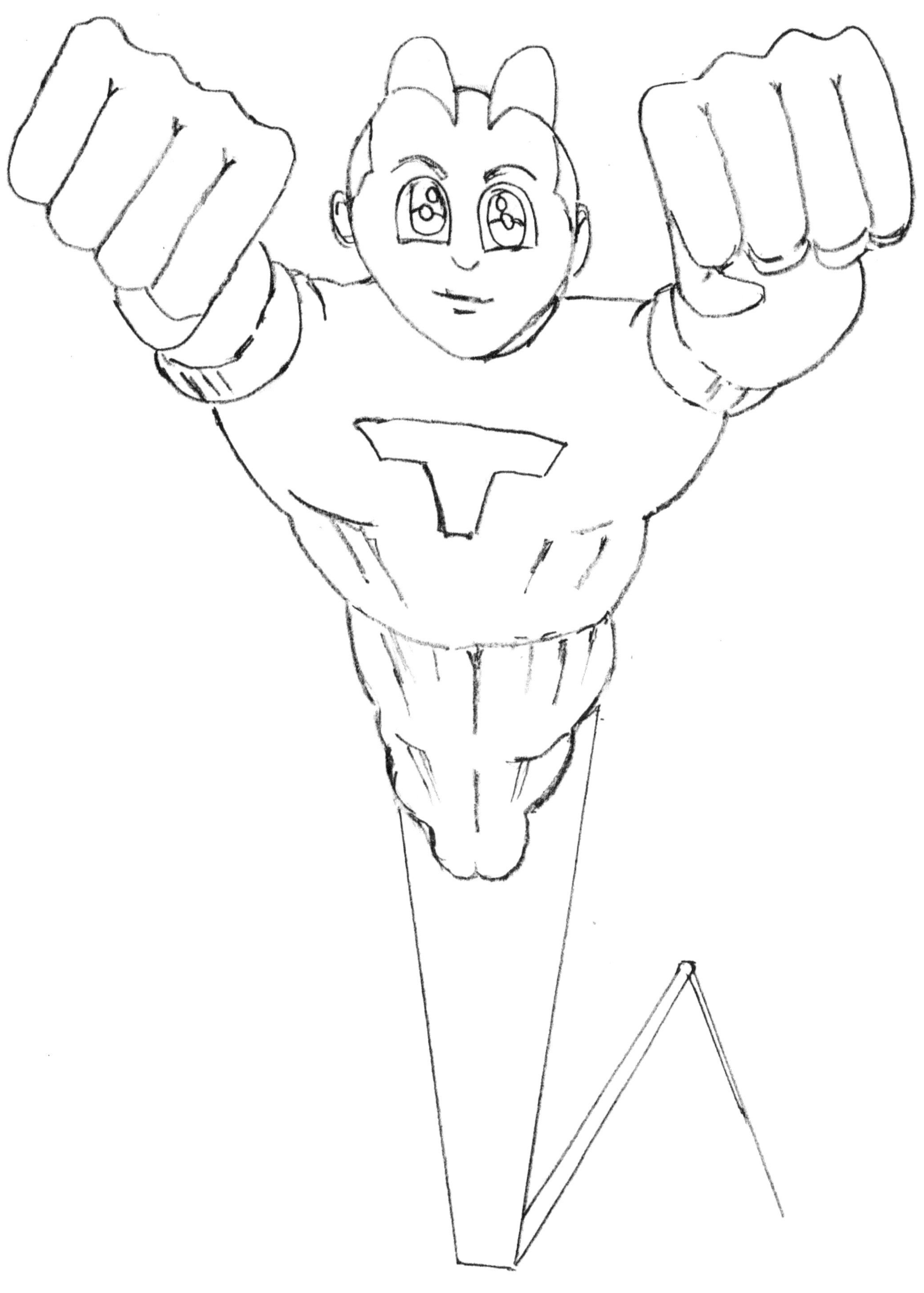

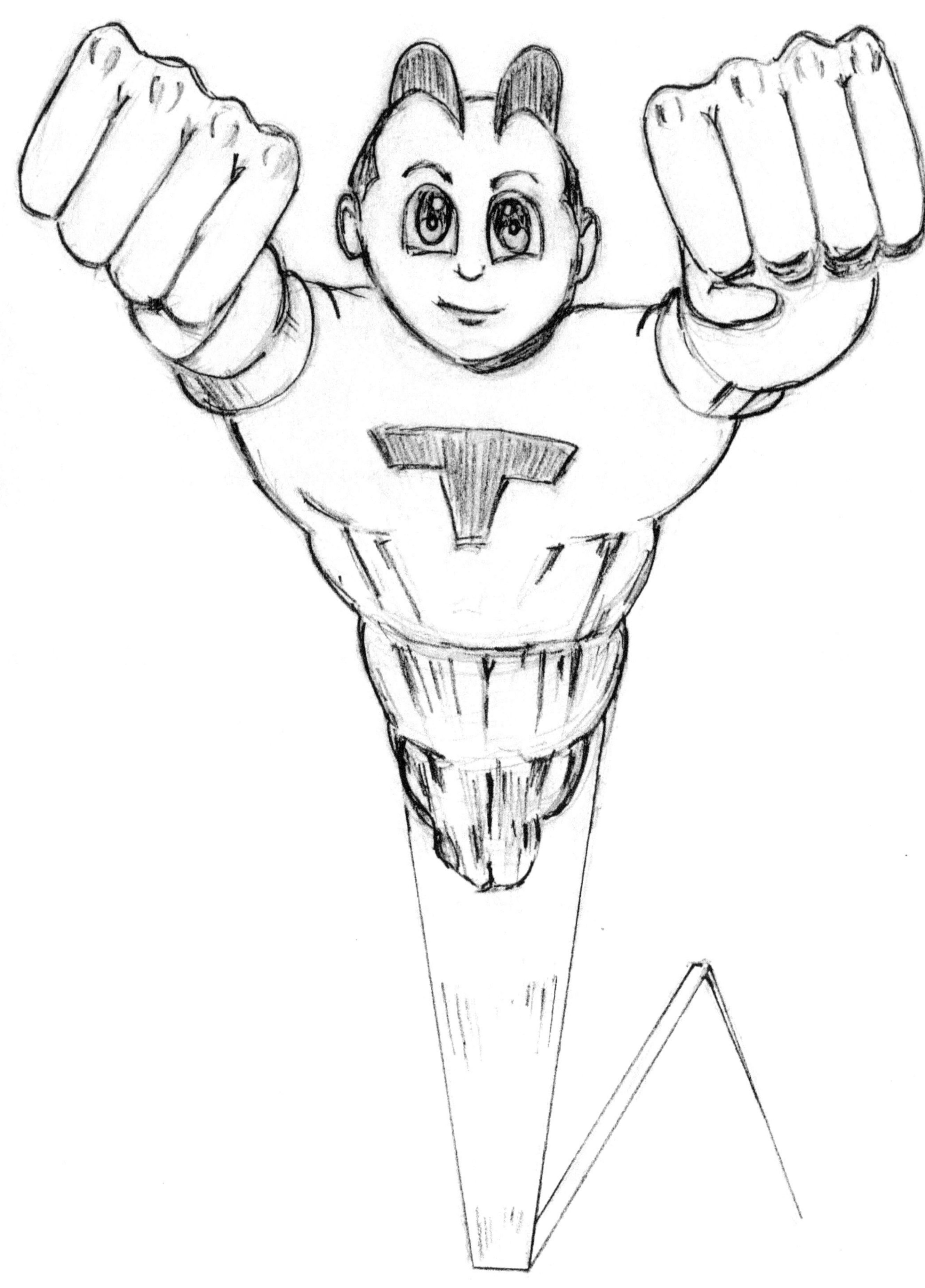

Mr. Clark

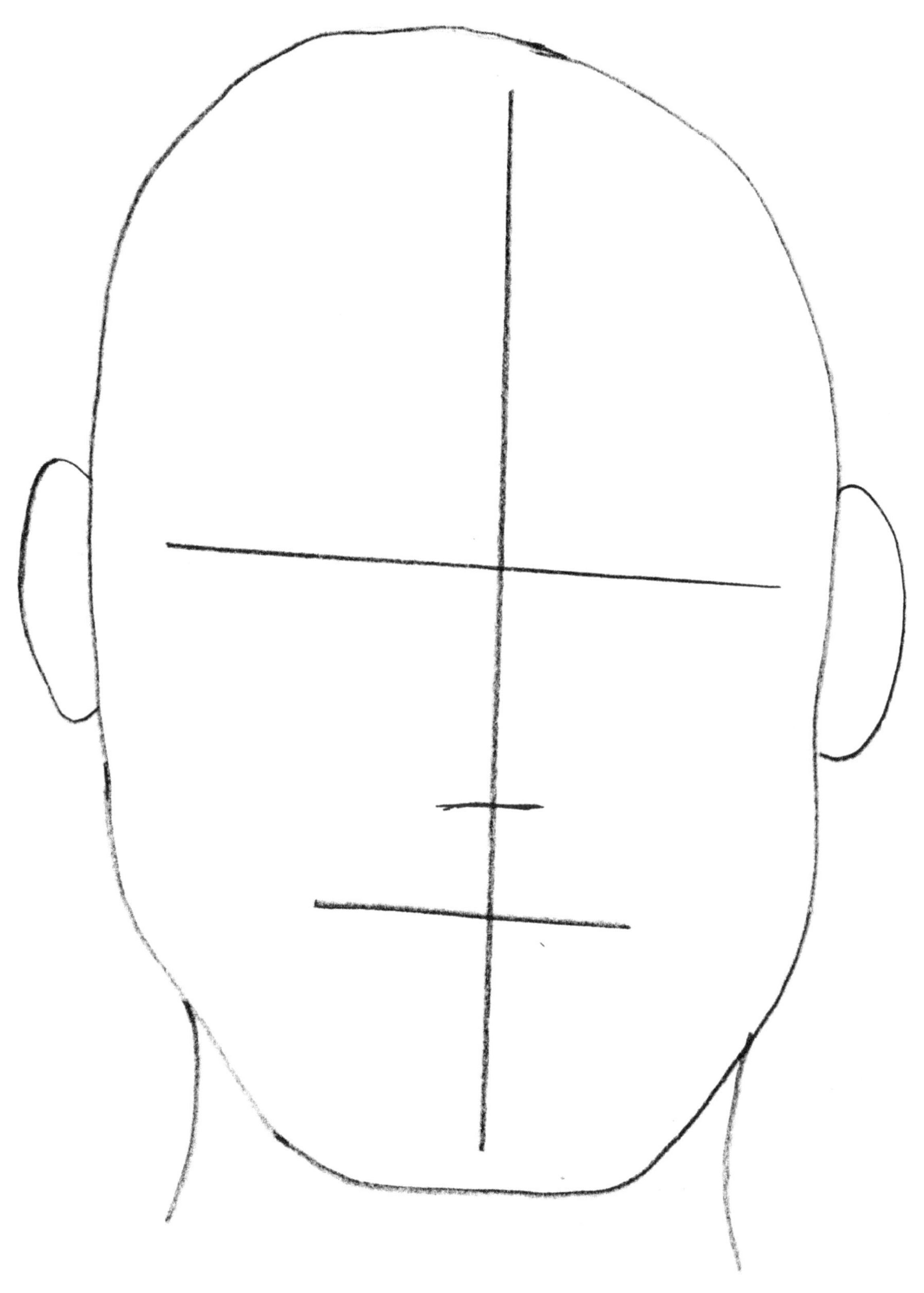

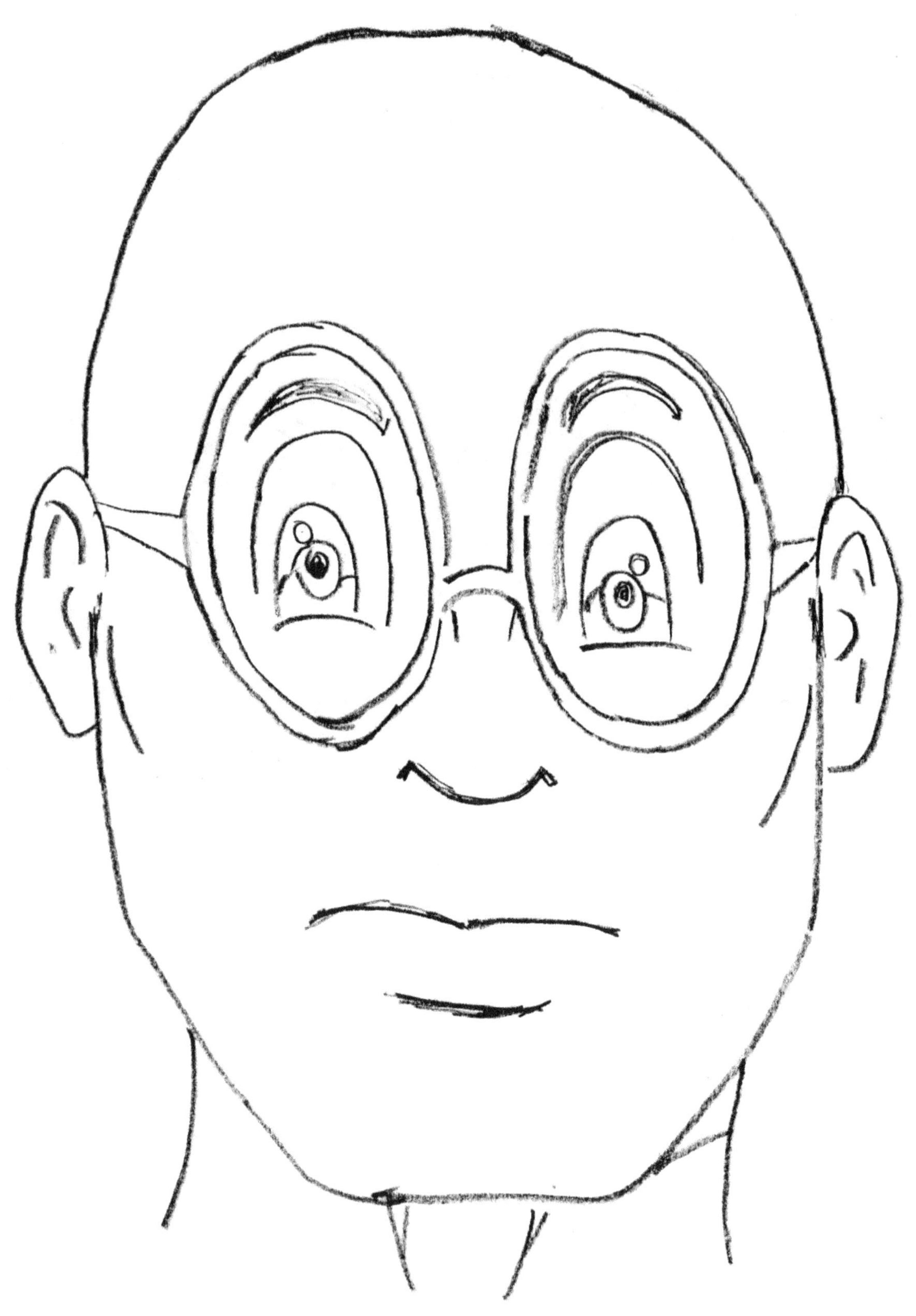

Giant Panda

Olivia

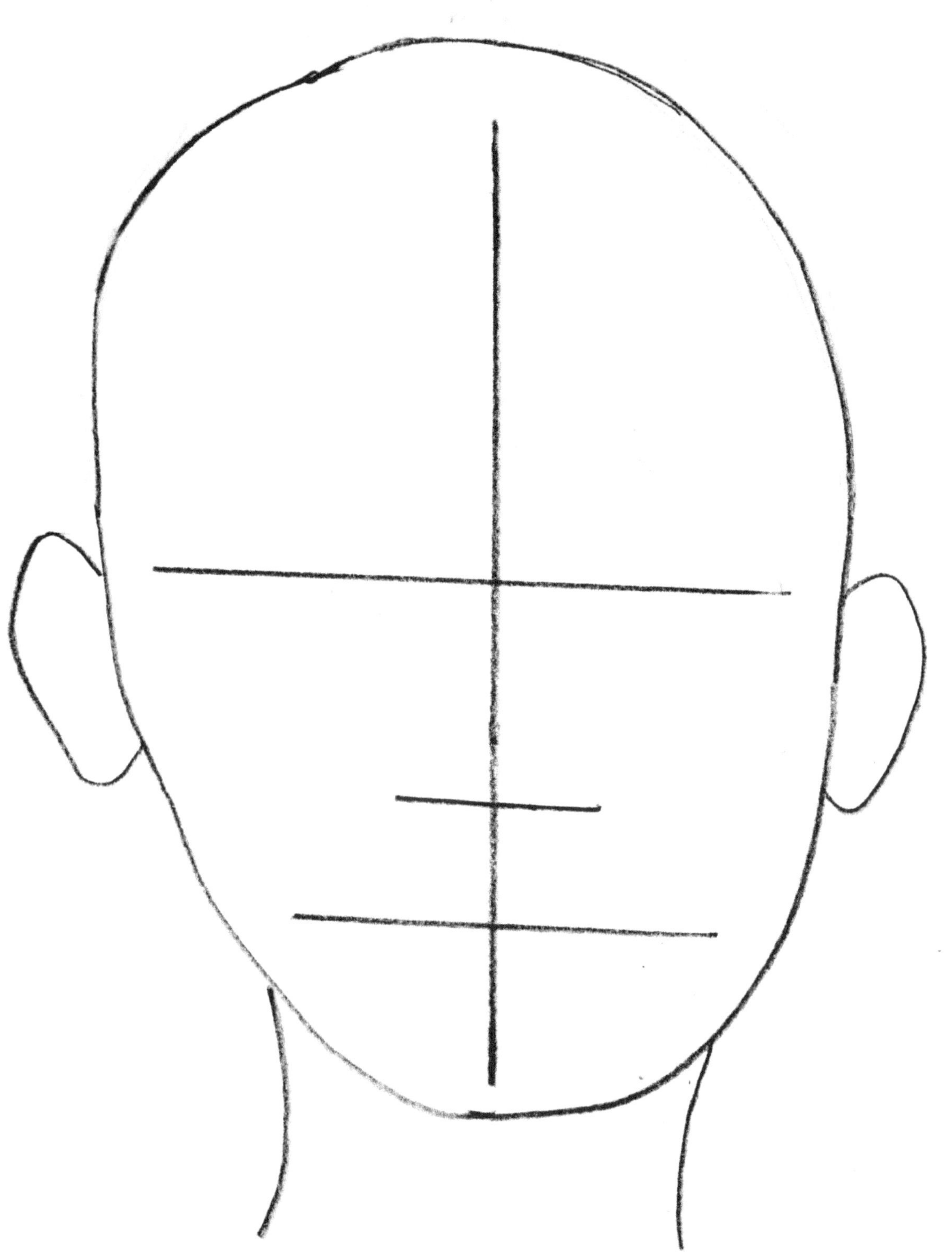

Rayland

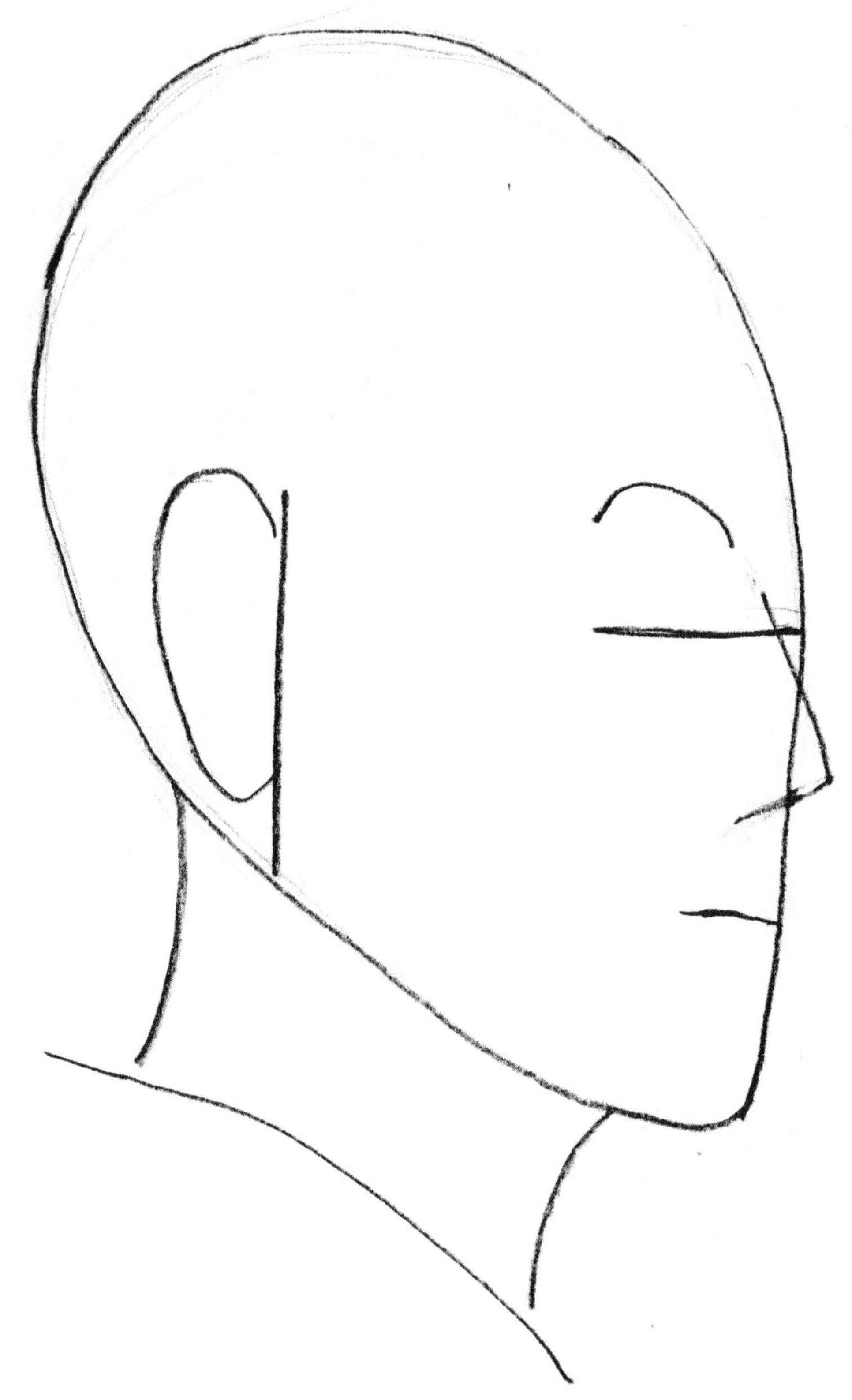

POOCHIE

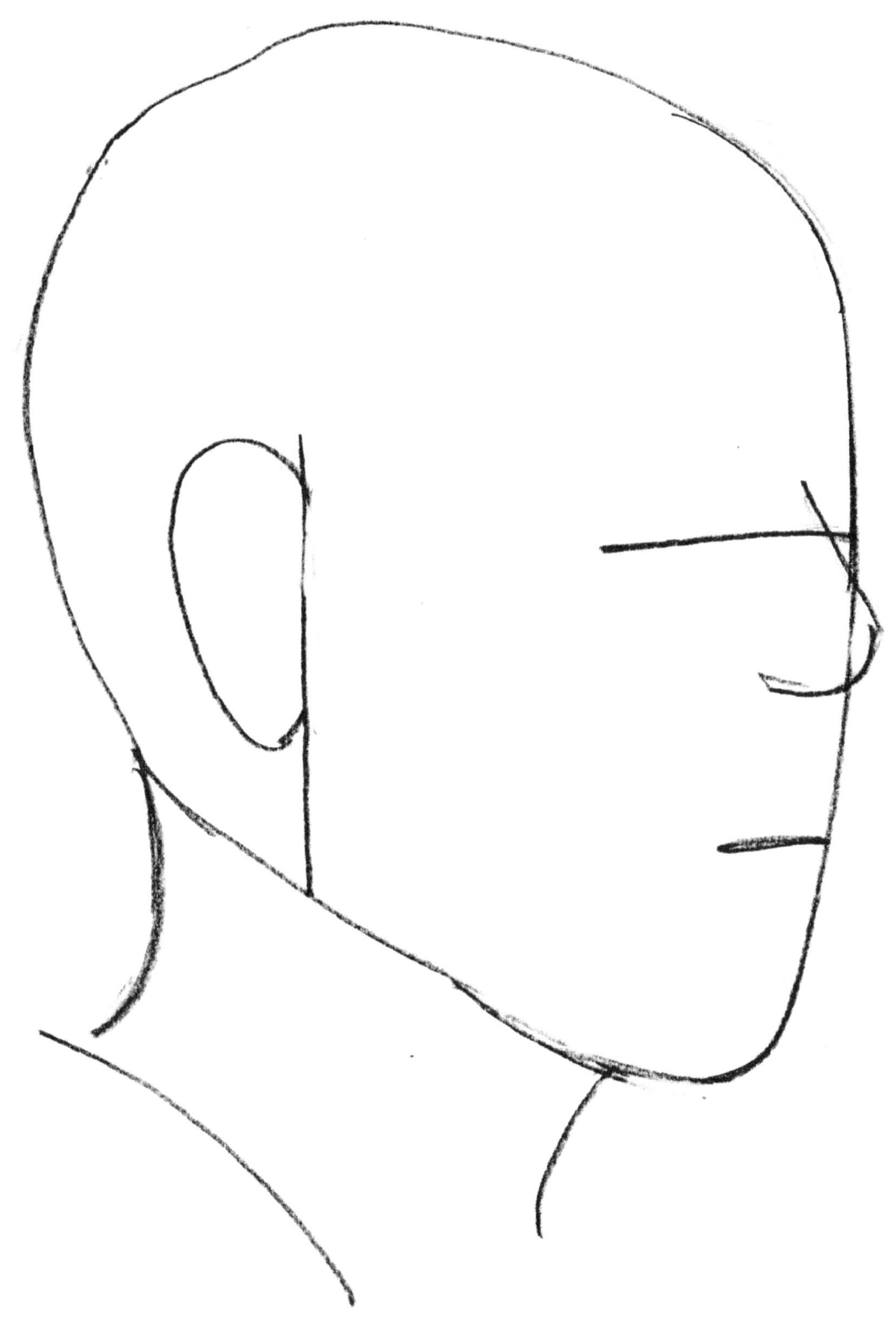

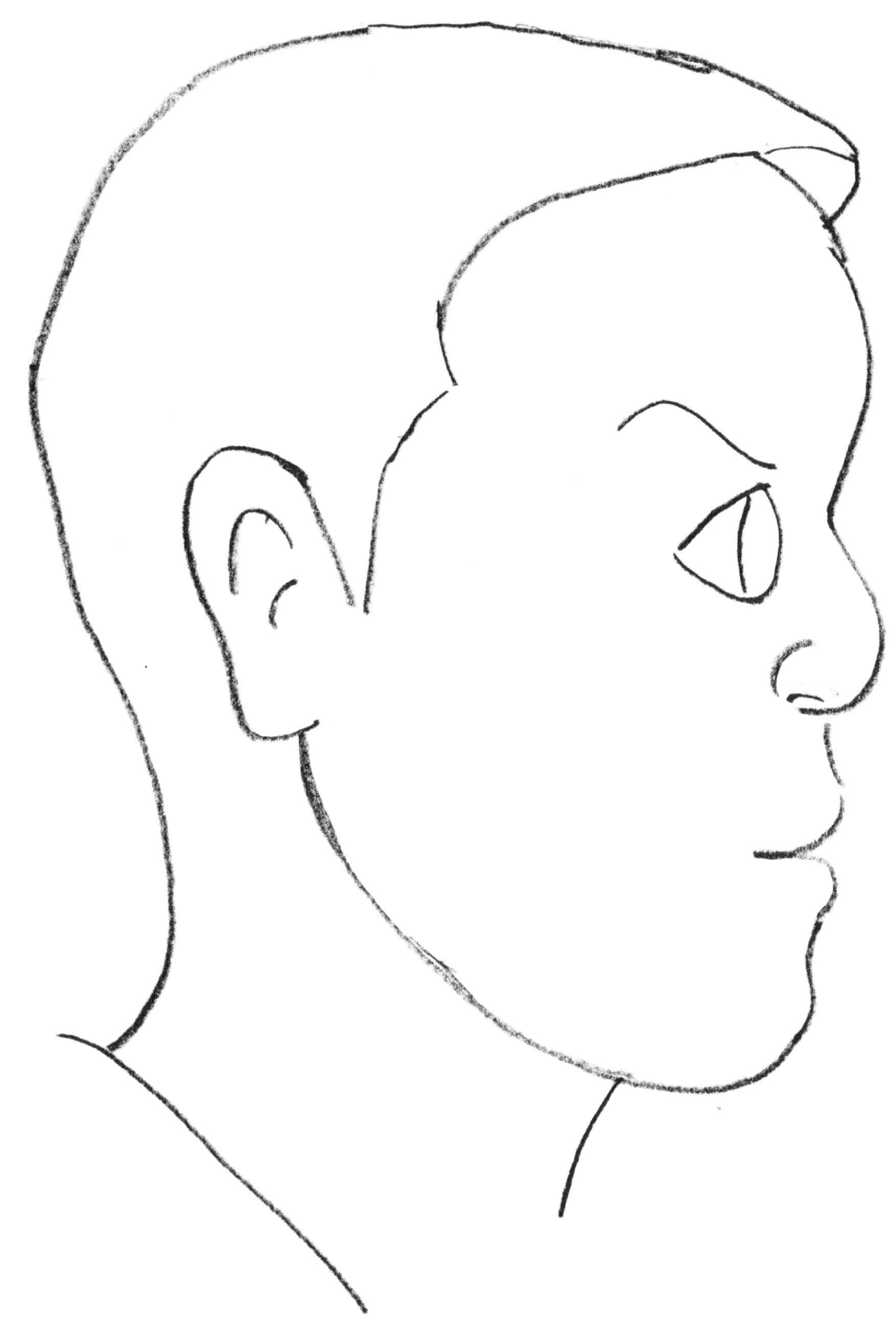

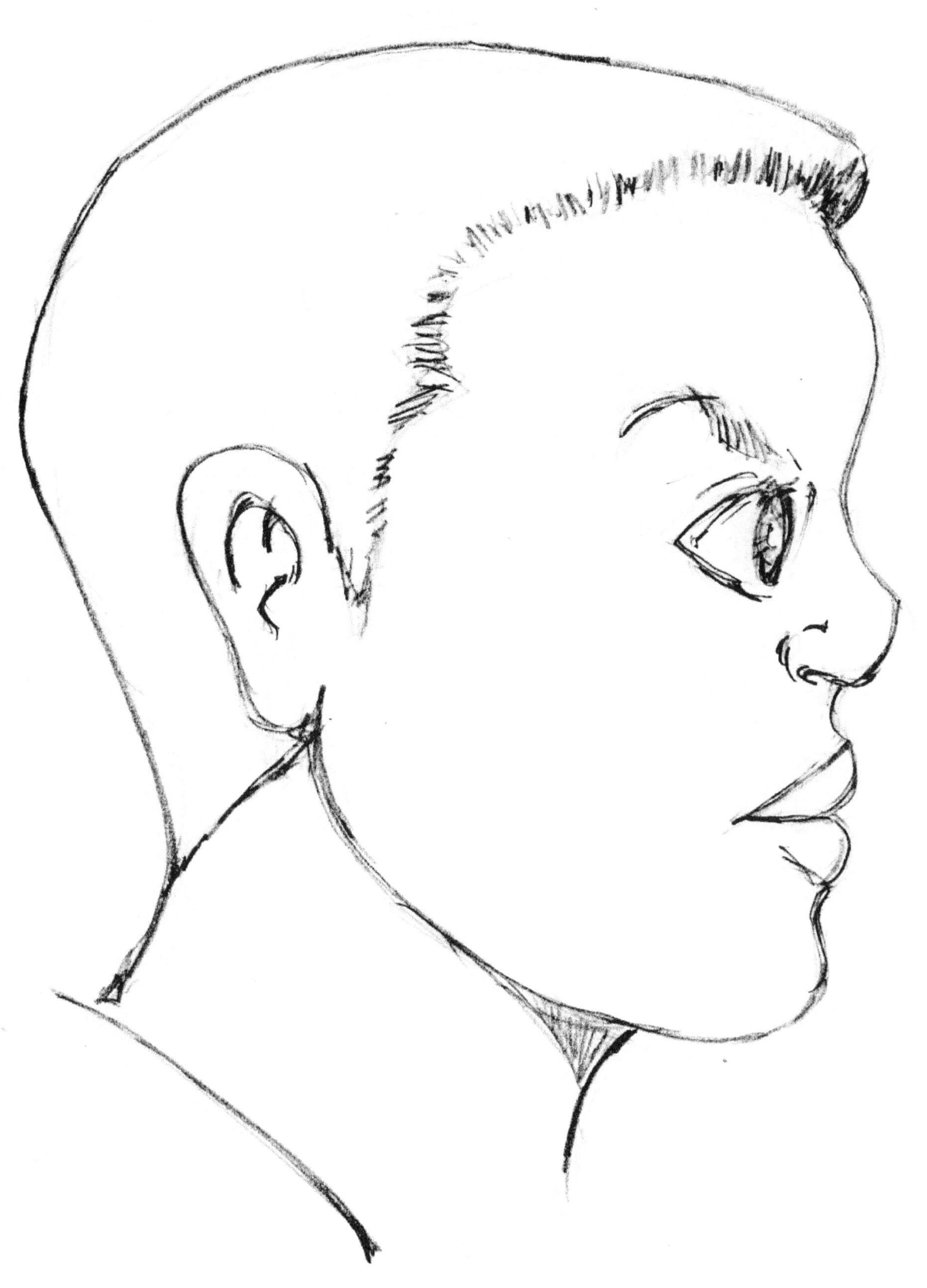

Zuzy

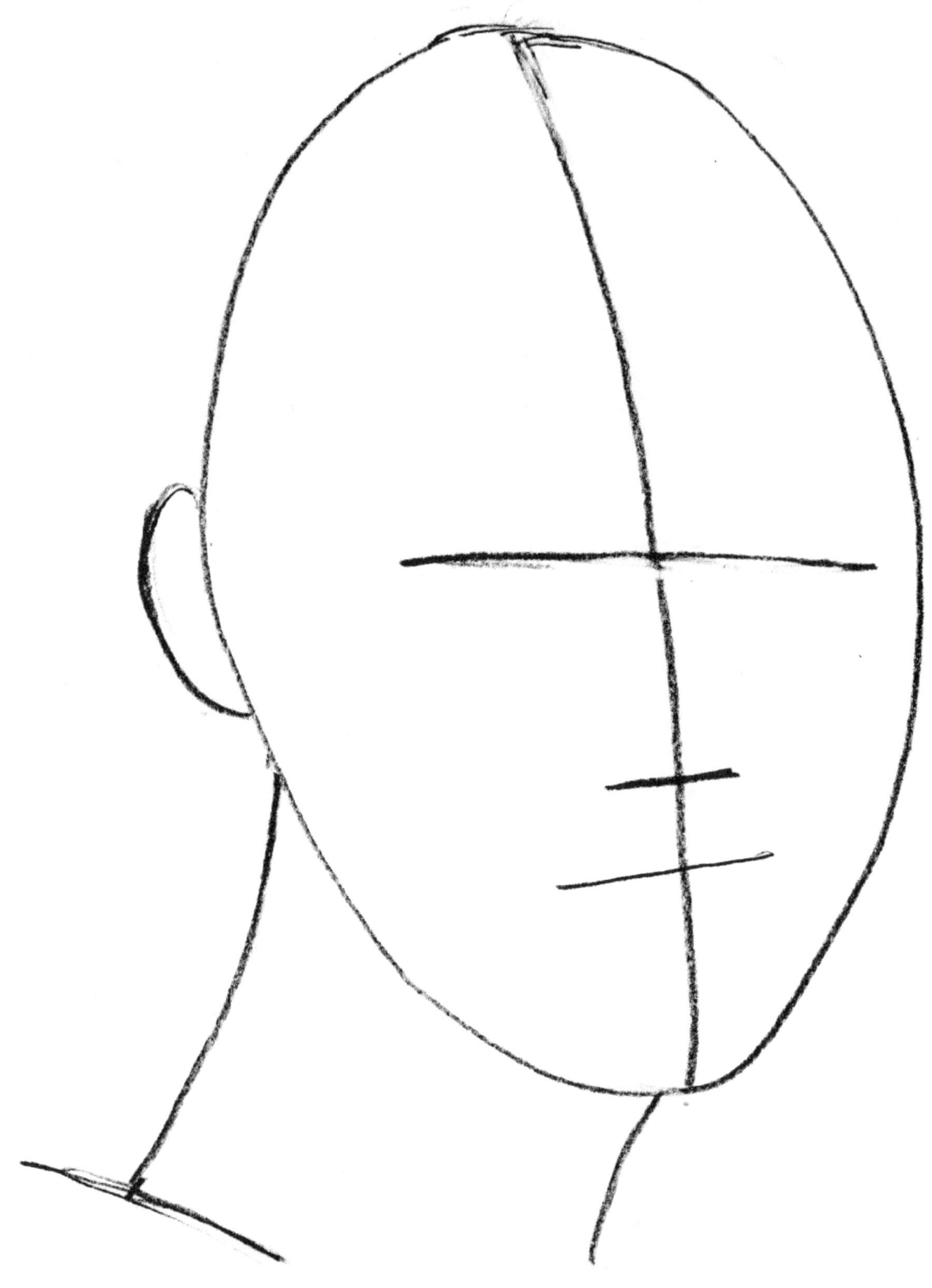

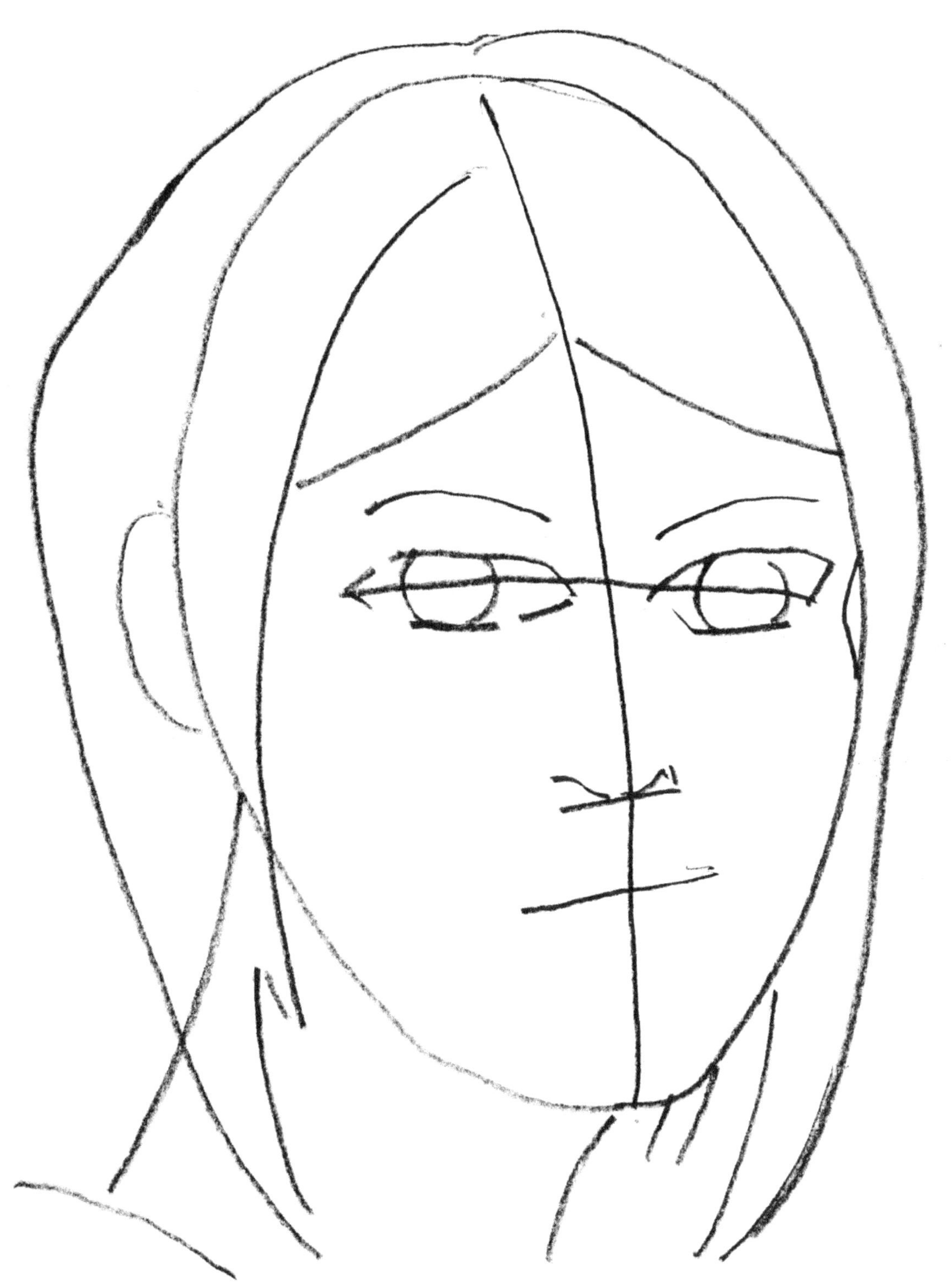

Delightful Duo

Vain Brain

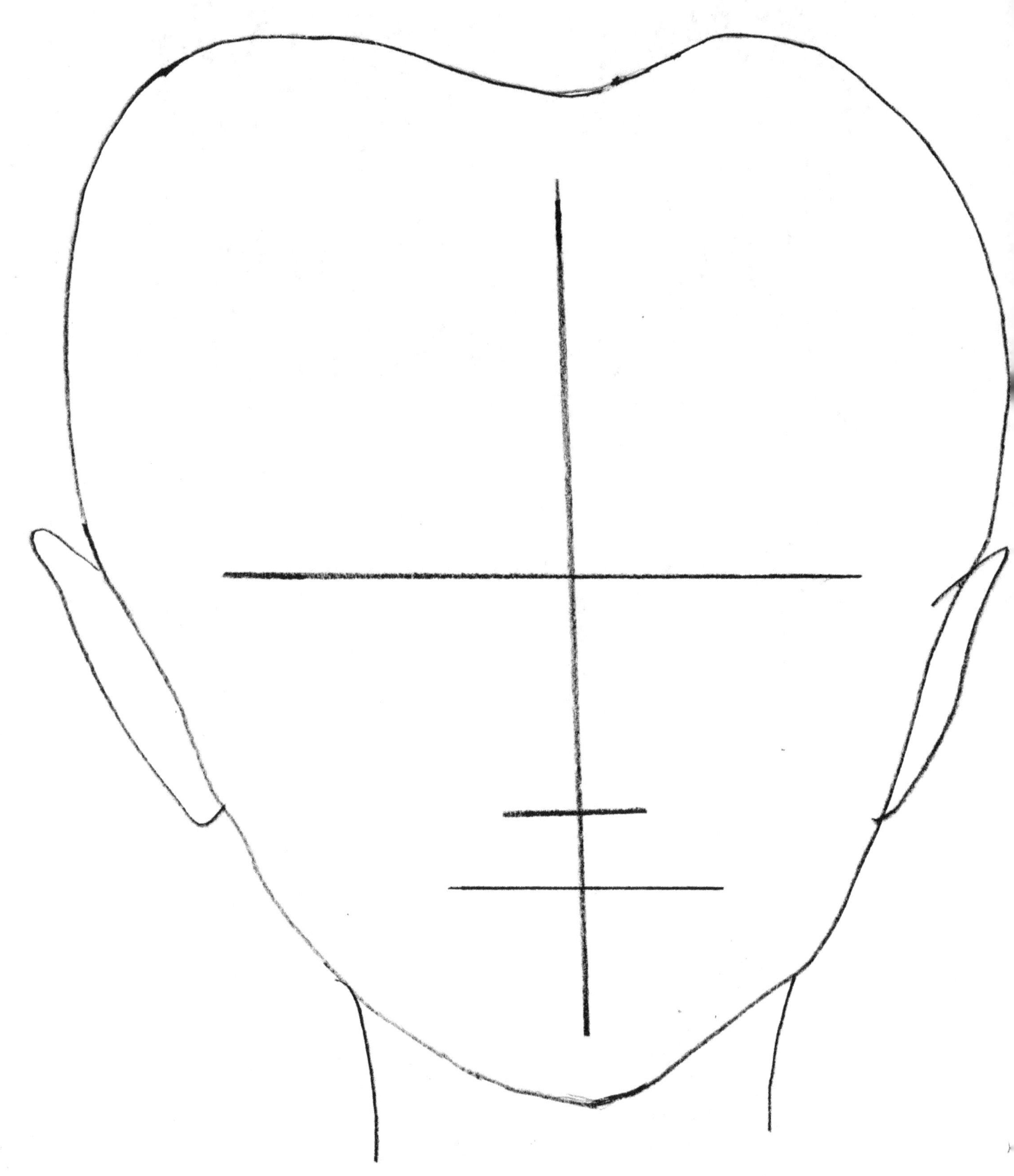

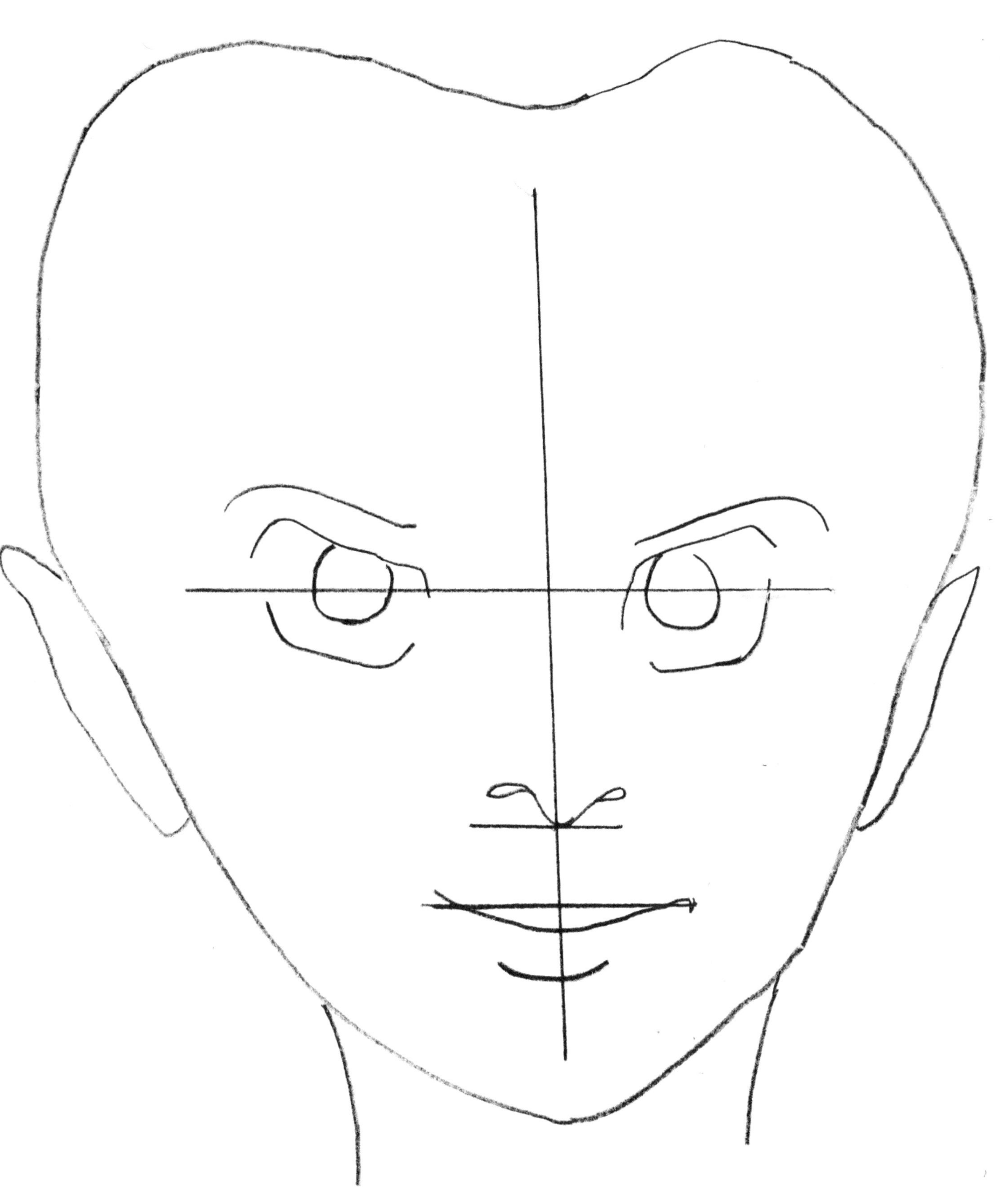

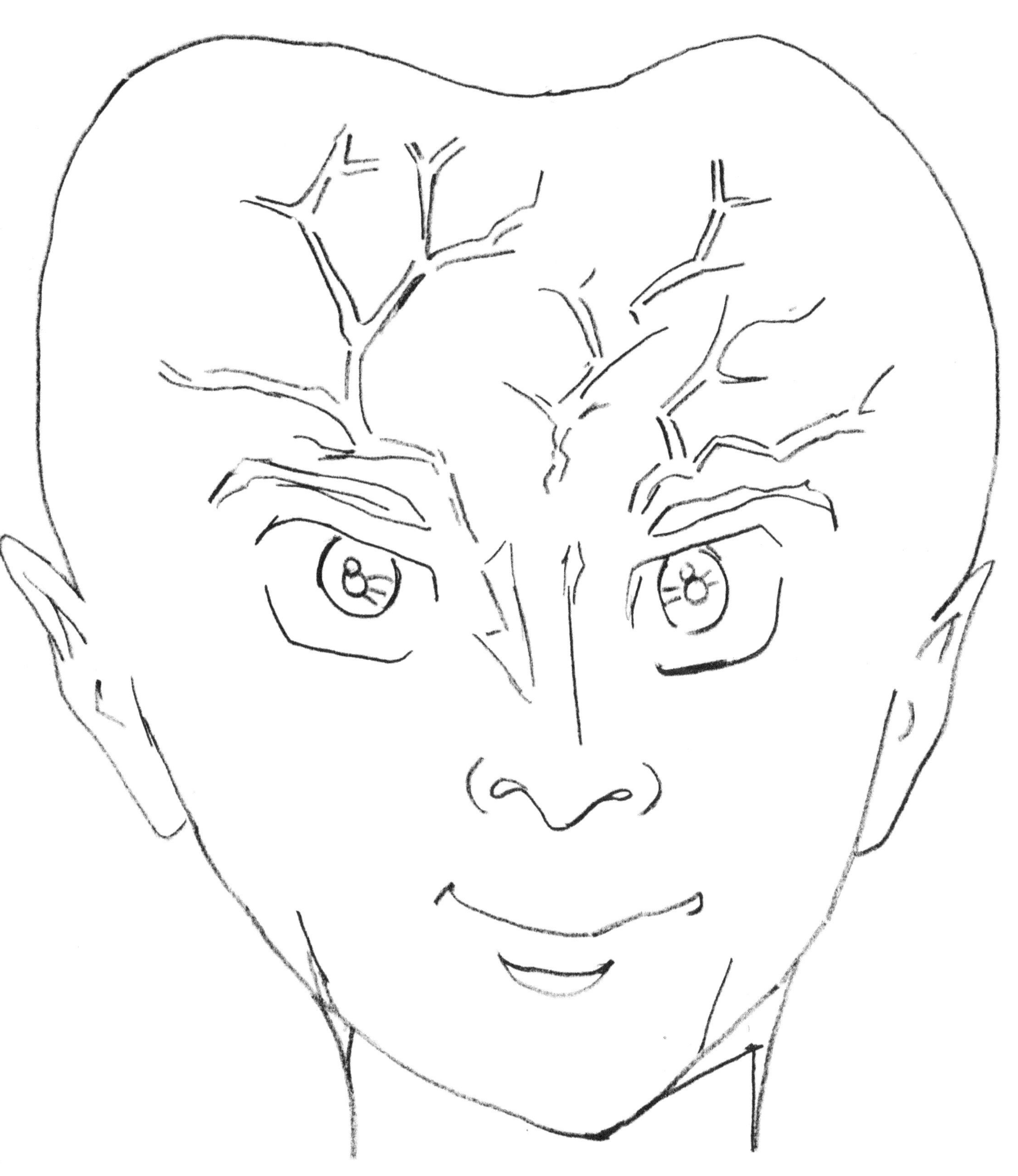

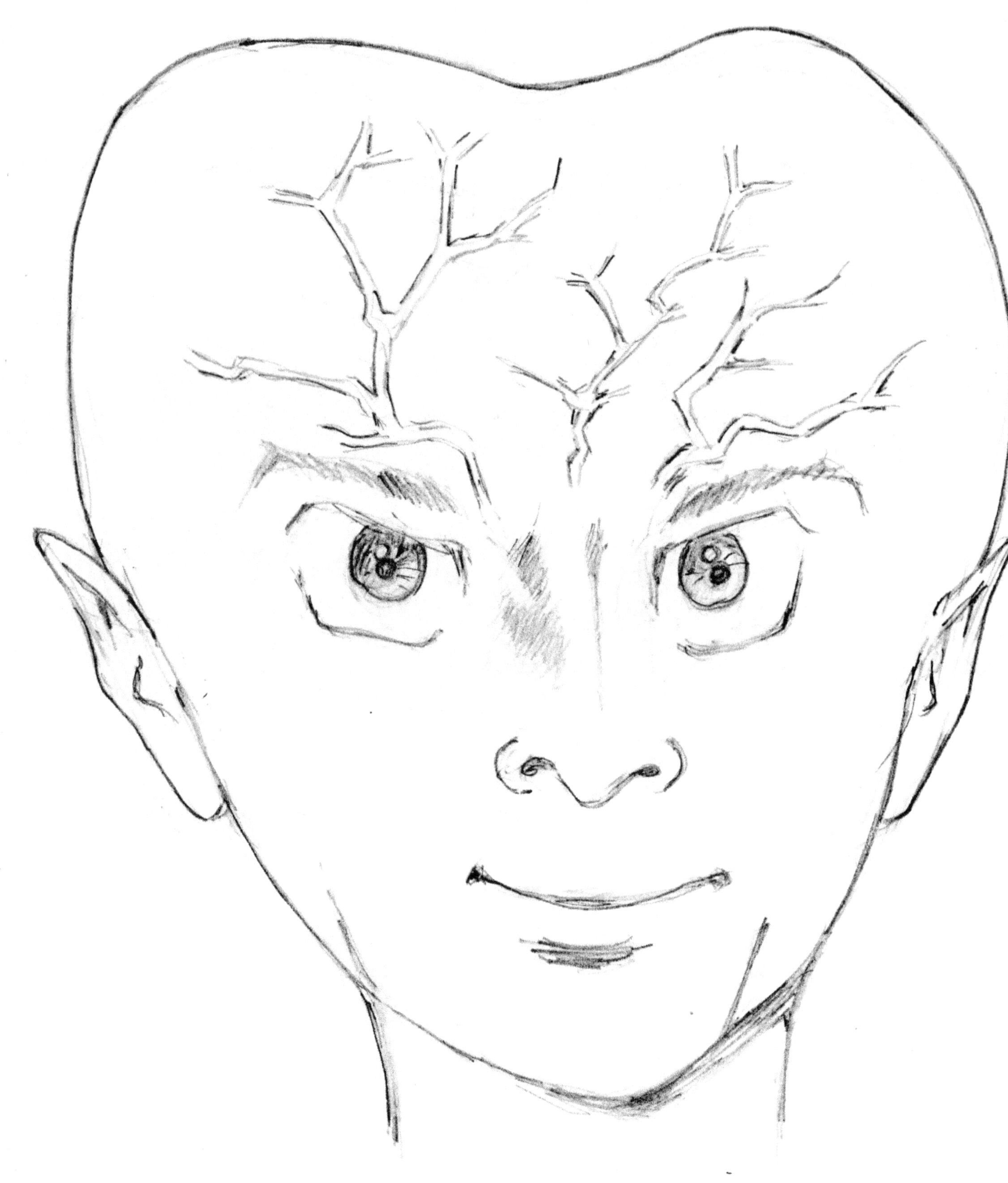

Comic Book Panel Pages

(You can draw directly on your comic pages or you can make copies, then draw on the copies.)

Name____ Issue____________ Page__________